W9-AFE-371

The
EAR
BOOK

by Al Perkins
Illustrated by
WILLIAM O'BRIAN

FRANKLIN PIERCE COLLEGE
LIBRARY
RINDGE, NEW HAMPSHIRE

A Bright & Early Book

CURR
PZ
7
.P429
Ear
1968

This title was originally catalogued by the Library of Congress as follows: Perkins, Al. The Ear book; illus. by William O'Brian. Random House © 1968 28 p. col. illus. (Bright and early books) A concept book about sound for beginning readers. 1 Sound I Title ISBN 0-394-81199-2 ISBN 0-394-91199-7 (lib. bdg.)

Copyright © 1968 by Random House, Inc. All rights reserved under International and Pan-American Copyright Conventions. Published in the United States by Random House, Inc., New York, and simultaneously in Canada by Random House of Canada Limited, Toronto. Library of Congress Catalog Card Number: 68-28464. Manufactured in the United States of America.

Ears

Our ears

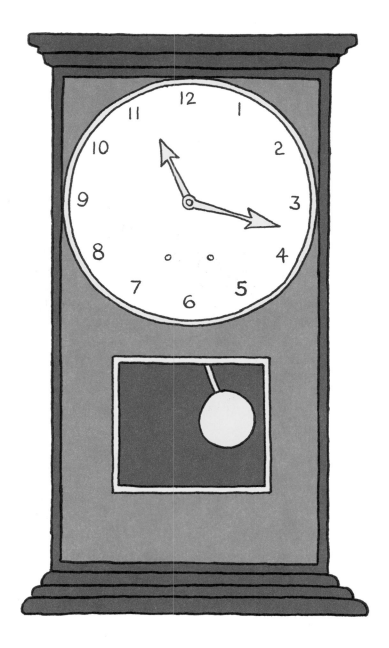

They hear a clock.

Our ears hear water.

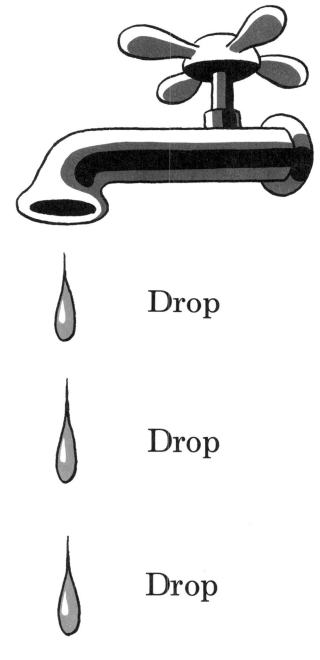

Drop

Drop

Drop

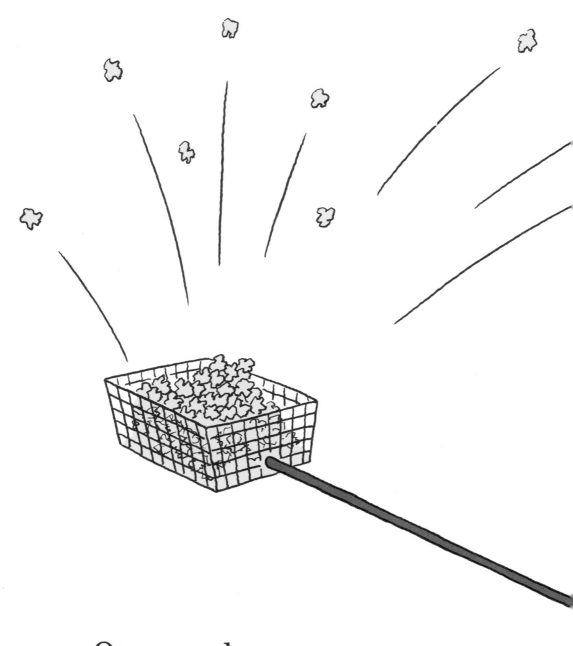

Our ears hear popcorn.

Pop
Pop
Pop!

Ears Ears
Ears
Ears

It's good.
It's good
to hear with ears.

Toot
Toot
Toot

We hear a flute.

We hear a Ding.
We hear a Dong.

We hear a Ping.
We hear a Pong.

We hear my sister
sing a song.

We also hear
my father snore.

We hear my sister
slam the door.

Boom! Boom!
Boom! Boom!

Dum! Dum! Dum!

It's good
to hear
a drummer drum . . .

and sister blowing
bubble gum.

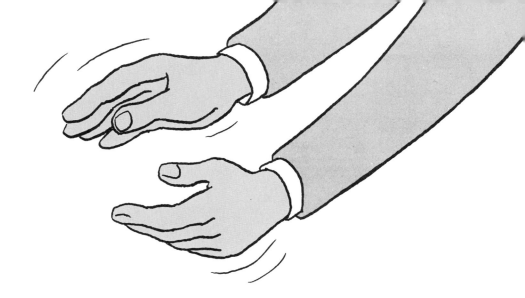

We hear hands clap

and fingers snap.

We hear feet
tap
tap tap
tap tap.

We hear a plane.

We hear a train.

It's good.
It's good
to hear the rain.

Ears. Ears. Ears!
We like our ears.
It's very good
to hear
with ears.

FRANKLIN PIERCE COLLEGE LIBRARY

00082237